Dear Amanda, Hannah & London,

Wishing you and your family much love and joy always!

Lisa R. Marks

JOY IS THE GREATEST GIFT

By Lisa Rey Marks

Illustrated by Eris Klein

Focus Friends, LLC
Fort Collins, Colorado

Book design and illustrations by Eris Klein
The illustrations in this book were created by combining traditional media (water colors, acrylics, and oils) on Adobe Photoshop and Illustrator.

The intent of the author is only to offer information of a general nature to assist in the quest for emotional and spiritual well-being. If you choose to use any of the information in this book, which is your constitutional right, you are responsible for your own actions. The author and publisher assume no responsibility for your actions or the actions of other individuals.

Published by Focus Friends, LLC
P.O. Box 271757
Fort Collins, Colorado 80527-1757
www.focusfriends.com

First Edition

Library of Congress Control Number: 2006904840

ISBN-13: 978-0-9786028-0-2
ISBN-10: 0-9786028-0-3

FOCUS FRIENDS, JOYANN, and associated logos, characters, names and distinctive likenesses are trademarks and/or registered trademarks of Focus Friends, LLC.

Printed in China by Palace Press International

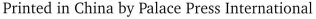

To my husband, Sandy Marks. My life with you is my greatest joy.
Thank you for your unconditional love and support.
I love you very much.

To my dear friend, Ann Nicholl.
You are the essence of Joyann.

~ L.R.M. ~

To my art students, from whom I learn so much.

And to my little nephews
Sergio, Liam, Adam, and Zachary.

~ E.K. ~

The sun is shining. It is a splendid day.
Allow me to introduce myself in a fun and gracious way.
My name is Joyann, and I am your Focus Friend.

We are most creative when
we are focused.
Creating joy is what I intend.

I have been given a precious gift that
I will share with you.

It helps us when we're mad,
and it helps us when we're blue.

At times, we feel mad. At times, we feel blue.
These feelings are okay as long as they are few.

Most days, let us celebrate joy!
Joy is the best choice for every girl and every boy.

Joy!

The best choice for
every girl and every boy.

Happiness!

Happiness!

So, open this gift and see what's inside.

Some of my favorite things I must confide.

The gift of joy is seeing beauty everywhere.

In cities and towns, smiles of people show they care.

Rays of sunshine gleam through the trees. Little birds nest in the branches and in the leaves.

Gardens of flowers colorful and bright.
Stars twinkling throughout the night.

Butterflies swirl and twirl in the air.

A nap with kitty by the fireplace
on a soft, cushy chair.

The gift of joy is enjoying days full of fun.
Sliding. Skipping. Tag - You're it! Run, Run, Run!

Jumping barefoot in puddles.
Squishing sand between your toes.
Blowing bubble gum all over
your cheeks, chin, and nose.

Playing with your favorite toys.
Eating snacks and making noise.

Dancing. Singing – "Fa, La, La."
Clapping and cheering – "Rah, Rah, Rah!"

For that time, giving thanks with all your heart.
Hugs and kisses each day with mom and dad.
A phone call to Grandma makes her so glad.

Summer evenings with neighbors.
Throwing little brother a ball.

Laughing with your best friends
for no reason at all.

Reading stories before bedtime.
Saying prayers and goodnight.

JOY

Safe and secure,
the sheets snug and tight.

There is no better way to spend a day, no better way to live. Joy is the greatest gift to receive and the greatest gift to give.

Joy is the best choice
for every girl
and every boy.

So, write your name on the present.
This gift has been passed - fill it with things
that will make your joy last!

Your Name:

My Joy List:

_____

_____

_____

_____

_____

_____

_____

_____

_____

Happiness ~ Joy ~ Happiness ~ Joy ~